JULIE
and the puppy

strations by José-Luis Macias S.
ginal story by J. Barnabé Dauvister
told by Jane Carruth

ock-a-doodle-do! . . . It's time to get up.
o hurry, Julie. Grandma has a big mug
chocolate waiting for you.

Goodness, look what
is sitting on my chair,
looking at my
breakfast! Isn't he a
dear little dog!

He must be a surprise present from Grandma. What a good idea! Now I have a holiday playmate. I will call him Muffin.

How hungry you are! Never mind, Julie will take care of you. Two curious little birds come and want to know more about the two new friends.

Now it's time for bed. Muffin will go to sleep in the basket which Julie has got ready for him. "We must sleep soundly so that we are ready for the lovely day we're going to have tomorrow," Julie tells him.

What an adventure! Petranella and Peter wonder what's happening to them. Muffin bites everything on sight — the ball, and then the cushion! There are feathers everywhere. Julie shakes her finger at him.

While keeping an eye on Muffin, Julie reads a story. Mervin, the hedgehog, walks around a little nervously. What would happen if Muffin were to mistake him for a ball?

Muffin has never seen a cow.
He thinks it is enormously big
and fat. What a funny
animal — to eat grass.

Woof! Woof! I'm not afraid of you.

Flossie the cat is bad tempered. She has scratched Muffin. "It's nothing," says Julie. "A nice clean bandage will make you feel much better."

"It is lovely to be cuddled by Julie," Petranella thinks. Muffin is a little jealous, and he waits in the pram for his turn.

"Pay attention," says Julie to her four little pupils. "This is a B.
B is for Butterfly. Muffin, you must join in the lesson too."

Muffin is in his new kennel. The butterfly, the snail, and the swallow have all come to welcome him.

Petranella, Julie and Mother Duck have come to see if all goes well. Muffin is guarding the house.

The holidays are over. Julie packs her bag to go home. Muffin is
going with her. They love each other so much they can't be
separated!

Published in the United States and simultaneously in Canada by Joshua Morris, Inc
431 Post Road East, Westport, CT 0688
Printed in Belgiur